Look for more

titles:

ATTENTION: ORGANIZATIONS AND CORPORATIONS
Most HarperEntertainment books are available at special quantity discounts for bulk purchases for sales promotions, premiums, or fund-raising. For information, please call or write:
Special Markets Department, HarperCollins Publishers,
10 East 53rd Street, New York, NY 10022-5299
Telephone (212) 207-7528 Fax (212) 207-7222

Surf, Sand, and Secrets

by Nancy Butcher
from the series created by
Robert Griffard & Howard Adler

HarperEntertainment
An Imprint of HarperCollinsPublishers
A PARACHUTE PRESS BOOK

A PARACHUTE PRESS BOOK

Parachute Publishing, L.L.C.
156 Fifth Avenue
Suite 302
New York, NY 10010

Published by
HarperEntertainment

An Imprint of HarperCollins*Publishers*
10 East 53rd Street, New York, NY 10022-5299

Chapter 1

Friday

Dear Diary,

Oops! Sorry about that. I didn't mean for you to get splashed. I've never written in you while I was on a yacht before. Actually, I've never even *been* on a yacht before! It's so cool!

A group of us from the White Oak Academy for Girls are here on a special school trip. That includes my sister, Mary-Kate, and a bunch of our friends from our class from the First Form. Diary, I'll never understand why they don't just call it the seventh grade. Oh, well . . .

A few of the boys from our brother school, Harrington, are here with us, including my weird and annoying cousin Jeremy Burke. Right now he's trying to catch fish off the back of the yacht. He said he couldn't wait for lunch.

I'm sitting at a table on the top deck, so I have a perfect view of everything. We're cruising through Hanalei Bay near the island of Kauai. That's one of the islands of Hawaii. We're on our way to Part Two of our summer vacation at the Hanalei Beach Resort!

Part One was spent in Hilo, which is on a different Hawaiian island. We played a survival game called Wild Hawaii, in which we had to live on the beach for twelve whole days.

Well, maybe not twelve days for me. I kind of got booted from Wild Hawaii on the very first day for not following the rules. Luckily my friends Elise Van Hook and Summer Sorenson got kicked out (accidentally on purpose) right after I did.

"I love this yacht!" my roommate, Phoebe Cahill, cried. She was sitting next to me and filming Elise and Summer, who were leaning against the ship's rail and waving.

Phoebe's been recording our whole trip. She says it's good experience since her dream is to be a journalist.

"Pssst. Ashley."

I glanced up. Dana Woletsky was leaning toward me from the next table. *This can't be good,* I thought. Dana isn't what I would call "a nice person."

"I was just thinking about the juicy secret I know about you," Dana said with a smirk.

I had no idea what Dana was talking about, but I could feel my cheeks turning red anyway. "What secret?" I asked.

"Don't worry," Dana said. "You'll find out soon enough." Her smirk turned into a big smile. "And you're going to get in so much trouble. I can't wait!" She tossed her shiny dark hair and turned back around to her own table.

I wasn't sure if Dana *really* knew a secret about me. You can never tell with her. Maybe she was just saying that so I'd be worried for the rest of the trip.

I think she's still angry that I won a hundred-dollar shopping spree in Hilo. You see, Diary, I volunteered at Wild Hawaii to help with chores even after I got kicked out. Our guide was so impressed he gave me a prize for teamwork!

Well, I'm not going to have time to worry about Dana. There's too much fun planned!

"Ashley, want to check out the resort's brochure?" Mary-Kate pulled a chair up to our table. She gave me a little smile, but I could tell that she wasn't exactly happy. She's bummed because she and her best friend, Campbell Smith, had a fight in Hilo. I hope they make up soon.

"Sure," I said, taking the booklet.

Phoebe leaned over my shoulder. "Look!" she said. "They have hula dancing! Hey, maybe I'll get to wear a grass skirt—just like Elvis Presley in my favorite movie, *Blue Hawaii*."

I giggled. Phoebe loved old movies. In fact, she loved anything vintage. At the moment she was wearing an orange 1950s bathing suit with a big yellow flower on one shoulder.

Elise brushed back her long brown hair. "Well, I can't wait to go surfing," she piped up.

"I'm already an expert surfer," Hans Jensen called over from the next table.

Hans is good at almost every sport. He lets everyone know it, too.

"I can't wait to try wave running," Mary-Kate said.

I smiled. "I'm going to try *all* those things," I said. "This is going to be an awesome week."

I looked at Summer, who was now sitting next to Hans. "Summer, what are you going to do first?"

But Summer didn't seem to hear me. She had her head buried in a magazine.

"Earth to Summer. Come in, Summer," I joked.

"Huh?" Summer's blond head snapped up.

"What are you reading?" I asked.

Summer held up the latest issue of *The National Inquisitor*. "I am so freaked out. There's the creepiest article in here."

"What's it about?" Mary-Kate asked.

"Aliens," Summer said. She leaned forward. "It says that just last week aliens were spotted hovering over Kauai. That's the island our resort is on!"

She pointed to a fuzzy picture of something that looked like a lit-up spaceship. It was hovering over a few palm trees. The headline read ALOHA, ALIENS!

A bunch of kids gathered around to look at the picture.

"Whoa," Julia Langstrom said.

"Cool!" Grant Marino added.

I rolled my eyes. They didn't really believe in this stuff, did they? I mean, the picture was a total fake.

"It says here that the aliens left a trail of purple shells along the beach," Summer added in a hushed voice. "And the trail pointed straight toward"—she gulped—"the Hanalei Beach Resort!"

I almost burst out laughing. What a joke!

"Hey, my cousin saw a spaceship when he was on vacation in Nevada," Seth Samuels said.

"Really? What did it look like?" Phoebe asked, putting down her video camera. She actually looked interested.

I frowned at my roommate. Why was she even asking something like that? Maybe she was just playing along. Or maybe it was because she was a journalist—always asking questions.

"It was spinning around and had lots of blinking lights," Seth replied. "You know. The usual."

Summer nodded seriously. "We see aliens back home in California all the time." She shuddered. "My friend's brother's surfing buddy almost got abducted once. They tried to take him right out of the water."

Everyone gasped.

"How can you guys believe in UFOs?" I asked.

Summer stared at me. "Ashley, the proof is right in front of your eyes!" She tapped a hot-pink fingernail at the article.

"Whatever you say, Summer." I sat back and folded my arms. "But I'm telling you. There's no such thing as aliens."

Dear Diary,

Here's the deal. I *want* to be happy at this resort. It's totally amazing. But how can I be happy when Campbell isn't speaking to me? She's not only been my roommate since the very first day Ashley and I arrived at White Oak, she's been my best friend!

We'd stay up for hours laughing and talking

about every subject on the face of the earth. She's actually the first girl I've met who knows more about baseball than I do.

And now she hates me because I made a stupid mistake.

"Is this place awesome or what?" Ashley asked as we walked into the huge lobby of the Hanalei Beach Resort.

I sighed. I knew Ashley was trying really hard to cheer me up, but it wasn't working.

"Did you catch the gigantic swimming pool and that amazing beach with the killer waves?" Ashley went on. "And that garden we just passed is incredible. It must have a million different kinds of tropical flowers in it!"

"Mmm-hmm," I said, staring at the floor.

Ashley looked at me sympathetically. "Hey, Mary-Kate, I know you're upset about Campbell. Do you want to talk about it?"

"I just don't know what to do," I said. "She ignored me the entire boat ride. She was too busy hanging out with her new best friend, Julia."

"Well, didn't you guys get to talk before we left Hilo?" Ashley asked.

"Barely," I said. "Just enough for her to tell me she doesn't want to speak to me . . . ever again."

"No way!" Ashley replied. "You guys are best buds. I can't believe she won't forgive you."

"I just wish I could take it all back," I said miserably. After all, I *did* do something really horrible to Campbell.

Back at Wild Hawaii, Dana Woletsky pretended to be my friend and told me a whole bunch of lies about Campbell. She even made it look as if Campbell had stolen something from me.

Dana was so convincing that I believed everything she said. And then I accused Campbell of being a thief and a liar.

"I apologized to Campbell a million times," I told my sister. "But I guess I can't blame her for being so angry."

"What are you going to do?" Ashley asked.

"I haven't figured that out yet," I answered, plopping into a chair near the front desk.

"Well, I'm going to check out the magazines in the gift shop," Ashley said. "Maybe we'll find the answer in an advice column or something." She walked over and pulled a magazine off the rack.

I glanced around the lobby, looking for Campbell. I didn't see her. A tall, good-looking man with short black hair passed by me. He had a fluffy white cat in his arms.

Hey, wait a minute! He looked just like . . .

"Oh, wow!" I cried. I jumped up and ran to my sister. "Ashley, do you see who that is?" I asked, tugging on her arm.

She glanced up from the magazine and wrinkled her nose. "Nope. I give up. Who is it?"

"It's Jake Nakamoto," I said. "One of the coolest, most amazing baseball players in the world!"

"Oh," Ashley replied. She went back to reading the magazine.

Okay, so maybe Ashley wasn't impressed by famous sports stars. But I was. And I knew someone else who would be, too. Campbell!

I scanned the lobby until I found her. She was jumping up and down, trying to see Jake over the huge crowd that was suddenly forming around him. Julia was with her.

Three beefy bodyguards waved the fans away from Jake. "Sorry, folks. Mr. Nakamoto is not signing autographs while he's at the resort," one of the guards said firmly. "No exceptions!"

Gee, that's harsh, I thought, frowning. I hurried over to Campbell.

"Jake Nakamoto is my number one favorite baseball player," she was telling Julia.

"Mine, too," I put in. "Can you believe he's staying here?"

Campbell glanced at me, then turned back to Julia. "Jake's batting average was .350 last year. Impressive, huh? And he hit thirty home runs!"

Okay, okay. I got the message. Campbell was ignoring me. But I wasn't going to give up.

"Hey, Campbell, remember when Jake hit that game-winning home run against Atlanta last season?" I asked.

This time she didn't even look at me.

"See that cat he's carrying? Her name is Snowball," Campbell explained to Julia. "Jake never goes anywhere without her. She's like his good-luck charm."

"Wow, you know a lot about Jake," Julia said.

"Yeah. I sure wish I could have his autograph for my collection." Campbell sighed. "It's such a bummer that he's not signing any."

A lightbulb went off in my head. *That's it!* I thought excitedly. *I'll get Jake Nakamoto's autograph for Campbell. She'll have to forgive me after that. We'll be best friends again for sure!*

There was only one problem. . . .

I glanced back at the tough-looking bodyguards surrounding Jake. How would I get past *them*?

Chapter 2

Saturday

Dear Diary,

This morning us grommets were  stoked to tackle those gnarly swells! (That's surfing lingo for we had our first lesson today!)

"Remember to lie flat on the board while you paddle in the water," our instructor, Lani, told us. "Ashley, you're up next."

No problem, I thought. I strapped on my life jacket. Then I lay on my board and paddled away from the beach. A few minutes later a humongous wave rushed toward me. I gulped.

"What do I do now?" I yelled to Lani.

"Try to float over the wave," Lani called.

"Okay!" I moved my arms as quickly as I could and tilted up the nose of the board.

"Uh-oh," I said. The board kept rising up, and up, and up until . . .

Crash! It flipped over and I went under the water. I popped up a second later.

Jeremy pointed at me from the shore. "Hey, Ashley! You got thrashed!" He laughed.

So what if I wiped out? I thought I did pretty well for my first time out.

"Good try!" Lani called. "Come on back now, Ashley."

I climbed onto the board again and paddled to the beach. I headed over to Mary-Kate and Phoebe, who were on the sand, catching rays.

"You okay, Ashley?" Mary-Kate asked.

I dropped my board on the sand and peeled a piece of seaweed off my leg. "Yeah. It was fun up until the wiping-out part."

"I wish we could stay in Hawaii forever." Phoebe sighed. Today she was wearing a bathing suit from the 1940s. It was really cute—navy blue with big white polka dots and a little pleated skirt.

"Me, too," I agreed, staring out at the clear blue ocean.

"I guess it's too bad you'll have to go home early, Ashley," Dana said behind me.

I turned around. Dana was in an expensive black tankini and designer shades.

"Sorry to disappoint you, Dana, but I'm not going anywhere," I replied.

Dana smiled. "If you say so." She wiggled her fingers at me and walked away.

"What was *that* about?" Phoebe asked.

"Dana thinks she knows some deep, dark secret about me." I shook my head. "She's really starting to get on my nerves. I mean, so what if I won the shopping spree. Get over it already."

"Don't worry, Ashley," Phoebe said. "I bet Dana's just messing with you."

Mary-Kate cleared her throat. "Actually, I'm not so sure about that."

I raised my eyebrows. "You're not?"

Mary-Kate bit her lip. She always does that when she doesn't want to tell me something. "See, uh, well . . . Dana *does* know a little something about you."

"Like *what*?" I asked. Then I narrowed my eyes. "And how do you know that?"

Mary-Kate turned bright red. "Because, um, I might be the one who told it to her."

Dear Diary,

I didn't think even Dana would stoop this low, but obviously I was wrong. Well, now it was totally time for me to come clean. I had kept the truth from Ashley for way too long.

I took a deep breath. "Remember how I thought Dana was my friend during Wild Hawaii?" I began.

"Yeeees," Ashley said slowly.

I sighed. "Well, we hung out a lot and told each other all kinds of stuff."

"Stuff like what?" Ashley asked, tapping her foot in the sand.

I hesitated. "Well . . ."

"Come on, Mary-Kate. Spill it now," Ashley demanded.

And then I told her. "Stuff like how you threw a party in your hotel room with Summer and Elise," I said.

Ashley's eyes almost bugged out of her head. *"Are you kidding me?"* she cried.

"Ashley had a party?" Phoebe cut in. "How come I wasn't invited?"

I quickly filled Phoebe in on the whole story. About how Ashley and her friends ordered tons of room service but didn't have any money to pay for it. And how they made a secret deal with the manager to work off the bill so our chaperones, Ms. Clare and Mr. Turnbull, wouldn't find out.

"Oh," Phoebe said.

Ashley dropped down on the sand and buried

her face in her hands. "Mary-Kate, how could you?" she said in a muffled voice.

"I just thought . . ." I began.

What *did* I think? I wondered. How could I ever believe I could trust Dana?

"What am I going to do?" Ashley wailed. "Dana's right. If Mr. Turnbull or Ms. Clare find out, they probably *will* send me home!"

"I'm really sorry," I said in a small voice.

Ashley glanced at me, but she didn't say a word.

"You know what?" Phoebe turned to Ashley. "There's a totally decent chance Dana won't rat on you."

"Yeah," I said quickly. "She's having way too much fun torturing you." *I hope,* I added silently.

Ashley was still quiet. Then she smiled a little. "It's okay, guys," she said. "No big deal. You're probably right."

I gave my sister a giant hug. "So you're not mad at me?" I just wanted to make sure.

Ashley sighed. "Just don't let Dana fool you again," she said. "And no more spilling my secrets to anyone. Got it?"

"Got it," I said, holding up one hand. "Never again. I promise."

"Okay, everyone!" Lani called out. "Back over

here. We're all going to practice surfing with a buddy now." She read some names off a list. "Julia Langstrom and Elise Van Hook. Jeremy Burke and Summer Sorenson. Mary-Kate Burke and Campbell Smith . . ."

I perked up. "Campbell and I are partners?" I whispered to Ashley. "This is great. Now she'll *have* to talk to me."

"Good luck, Mary-Kate," Ashley said as I grabbed my board.

I walked across the hot sand to where Campbell was standing with her board. "Hey," I said extra-cheerfully.

"Hi," Campbell said.

Okay, not overly friendly, but it's a start, I thought.

"So what do you think of the class so far?" I asked.

Campbell shrugged. "It's fine."

All right! I cheered. *We're having a real conversation. Almost.*

"So maybe—" I began.

"Look," Campbell cut in, "I'm sorry, but I don't really feel like talking right now."

My heart sank. "Campbell, you know I'm sorry for what happened back in Hilo. Can't we just start

16

over?" I asked. "We're best friends, right?"

There. It was probably some kind of record. Two apologies in about two minutes. One to my sister and one to my roommate.

Campbell was silent for a minute. Was that a good sign? Was she finally going to forgive me?

"Mary-Kate," Campbell began, "you believed Dana instead of me. You accused me of stealing. A real best friend wouldn't do that."

She stared directly into my eyes. She totally meant what she said. And I didn't realize it until right then, but Campbell wasn't just angry with me. She was really hurt.

"But . . ." My voice trailed off. What else could I say? Campbell was right. Best friends don't turn their backs on each other. And that's exactly what I did.

We paddled our boards out into the water in silence. In fact, we didn't say a word to each other for the next half hour—even when we both wiped out at the same time.

That's when I decided I was going to start Operation: Autograph the second we got back to the hotel.

I had to prove to Campbell that I care about her. That she can trust me again. That I really am her best friend.

Two of a Kind Diaries

Dear Diary,

When I got to my room I threw on a pair of shorts and a tank top over my bathing suit and hurried back down to the lobby with a pen and a piece of hotel stationery.

I was on a mission. I was going to get Jake's autograph for Campbell no matter what it took.

I checked the pool, the gym, the gift shop, the ballroom, and the Luau Lounge.

No cat-carrying baseball players.

Finally I peeked into the Coconut Room, one of the fancy restaurants at the resort. It looked like the kind of place someone famous would have lunch.

Score! There was Jake, sitting at a corner table with one of his bodyguards.

I knew the bodyguards had said no autographs. But once they heard my story, I was sure they would let me talk to Jake.

I quietly made my way through the tables in the restaurant. *I'm only a few feet away from him*, I thought excitedly. *I can't believe how easy this—*

"Jake Nakamoto!" a woman cried suddenly. "It's *him!*"

"Uh-oh," I said under my breath.

Loud footsteps sounded behind me. A large group of tourists ran by, waving pens in the air.

They swarmed around Jake's table. "Jake! Jake, can we have your autograph?" one of them shouted. "Look this way, Jake! Say cheese!"

A camera flashed.

One of Jake's bodyguards jumped up from his seat and stood in front of Jake. "Mr. Nakamoto is trying to relax. No autographs," he barked. "And no more pictures, please."

I squeezed through to the front of the crowd. "Excuse me, sir," I said to the bodyguard. He must have been seven feet tall.

The bodyguard glared at me. "What?"

"Well, I know you said Jake isn't signing autographs," I said quickly. "But I have a total emergency. My best friend isn't talking to me. And I just know she'll be my friend again if I get Jake's autograph for her."

"*That's* your emergency?" the bodyguard asked.

I nodded. "So I'm sure you can understand how important this is." I held out my pen and piece of paper.

The man shook his head. "Jake's not signing autographs on this trip."

"But—" I started.

"Sorry, kid," he said. "No exceptions."

"Thanks anyway." I walked away, feeling discouraged. Obviously Jake's bodyguards didn't care that I had lost my best friend.

I glanced back at Jake. Of course he deserved to relax in Hawaii. Everybody did.

But he seemed so nice on all those TV interviews Campbell and I watched together back home. I bet if I told *Jake* my story, he'd understand. He might even give me an autograph.

It was time for Plan B: Figure out a way to sneak past those bodyguards!

Dear Diary,

The weirdest thing happened last night. After dinner Summer and Elise invited a bunch of us to watch a DVD in their room. (That's not the weird part. I'll get to it in a second.)

"Okay, is everyone here?" Elise asked.

"Yes!" Summer, Campbell, and I said together.

"Present," Phoebe answered.

"Can we just start the movie now?" Dana asked impatiently. "I have an early spa appointment in the morning."

"Wait a sec, Mary-Kate isn't here yet," I pointed out.

Just then the door burst open and Mary-Kate came rushing in. "Sorry I'm late!" she said. "What are we watching?"

"You're just in time," Elise replied, popping in the DVD.

"The movie is called *Return of the Killer Pod People*," Summer announced. "It's based on a true story about aliens."

"Oh, boy," I muttered. All through dinner Summer had been going on and on about aliens.

 She'd heard some weird guy talking in the lobby about that *Inquisitor* article. According to him, groups of fat little green men had been seen invading the beach.

Give me a break.

Mary-Kate squeezed into an empty space next to Campbell.

Then Campbell did something really mean. She got up and sat next to Julia on the other side of the room!

Poor Mary-Kate, I thought. *She didn't deserve that.*

I had an idea. Campbell and I always got along pretty well. Maybe *I* could talk to her.

I got up and walked over to the bowl of popcorn,

which was on a table behind Campbell. "Hi," I whispered as the movie credits flashed onto the screen.

Campbell turned around. "Hey, Ashley. What's up?"

"Look, maybe this is none of my business," I said, keeping my voice low. "But Mary-Kate feels really terrible—"

Campbell looked back at the screen. "I know, but—"

"She made a huge mistake," I said. "You're her best friend, though. And best friends forgive each other, right?"

"Shh!" Dana said. "I can't hear the movie, Ashley."

I really wanted to snap back at Dana. After all, I was in the middle of something important here! But I was a little worried that she might tell my secret if I did. So I kept quiet.

"Ashley, you're blocking our view," Summer complained. "The aliens are flashing messages from their hideout. I can't read them."

"Just think about it," I whispered to Campbell. I sat next to Mary-Kate to watch the movie.

There was a giant cornfield on the screen. A farmer stood in the field, gazing at the night sky. Creepy music filled the room.

Suddenly a big spaceship with flashing colored lights appeared. The farmer screamed. Then he threw down his pitchfork and started to run.

Elise screamed, too. "He doesn't have a chance! They're going to get him!"

"You can't outrun aliens," Summer said. "That's a total fact."

A huge beam of bright blue light came down from the spaceship and swooped up the farmer.

"They're going to do experiments on him," Summer said. "But not yet. Keep watching."

The scene changed to a deserted beach, where a young couple was taking a romantic walk.

The spaceship appeared again and beamed the woman away.

Summer passed over the bowl of microwave popcorn. "Can you believe that this actually happened?" she whispered.

"Not really," I muttered.

"No, it did," Elise whispered. "I read all about the making of this movie in *Hollywood Gossip* magazine. They interviewed the director, who swears that it's a true story!"

I munched on some popcorn and watched the UFO land in a desert somewhere. Creepy green men with three huge red eyes in their heads emerged and began to search for something. Everywhere they went they left a long trail of yellow slime.

"Gross," Mary-Kate said.

"Ew!" Julia cried.

"Check this part out," Summer said, pointing to the TV. "They're making patterns with those little purple glowing rocks."

Phoebe frowned. "Wait a second, Summer," she said. "Didn't that article you were reading say something about little purple shells . . . ?"

I turned my face away from the screen, trying not to laugh. I hoped Phoebe was just saying that as a joke.

Something outside the window caught my eye. Bright, flashing lights were flickering in the darkness.

Mary-Kate noticed them, too. "What's that?" she said.

Everyone turned to look. The lights kept flashing on and off. They seemed to be getting closer and closer.

Suddenly a huge rush of air blew the curtains straight up into the air.

"Oh, no!" Summer shrieked, dropping the bowl of popcorn. "It's the aliens! They're coming to get us!"

Chapter 3
Sunday

Dear Diary,

Guess what happened next, Diary.
Elise started screaming. So did everybody else.

But I kept my cool. I had to see what was out
there, though. I jumped up and hurried to the window to get a closer look.

"Ashley, don't!" Elise cried.

"They'll kidnap you and freeze you and stick
you in a giant test tube!" Summer added. "Ooh, I
can't watch." She buried her head under a
pillow.

I peered out the window.

"Take us to your leader!" an eerie-
sounding voice called.

"Nooooo!" Elise shrieked.

"Shh!" I said, motioning with my hand.

"Leader . . . leader . . . leader . . ." the
voice echoed.

I frowned. Hey, wait a minute. That sounded
like . . .

"Jeremy, is that you?" I yelled.

"No," the voice mumbled from the bushes.

I looked closer. Sure enough, Jeremy and Hans were hiding in some flower bushes under the window. They were waving around big flashlights and turning them on and off.

I opened the window wider and leaned out. "You two are *so* dumb!" I shouted.

"Not dumb enough to believe there was an alien spaceship outside your window," Jeremy said. He and Hans cracked up.

My friends gathered around the window.

"Don't make fun of aliens!" Summer burst out. She threw a handful of popcorn at the boys. Hans ducked. But Jeremy caught some popcorn and stuffed it into his mouth.

"Let's just finish the movie," I said.

But no one wanted to watch anymore. Not even Phoebe. They were too busy talking about aliens again.

Diary, I cannot tell you how sick I am of the whole subject. Has everyone gone nuts? Even Mary-Kate was getting into it. Luckily, the next day at lunch we had something else to talk about.

Phoebe, Elise, Summer, and I were sitting at a table in the hotel coffee shop. The waitress brought our food, and we all dug in.

"This veggie burger tastes really weird, you

guys," Phoebe said after a few bites.

Phoebe's totally serious about her veggie burgers. She's doing the whole vegetarian thing. She's even got a rating of the diners near  White Oak based on the quality of their veggie burgers. Phoebe slid her plate over to me. "Here, try it."

I picked up the burger and tasted it. "Seems okay to me," I said. "Except it needs more ketchup."

"Try it again," Phoebe urged me.

I took another bite. "You're right," I said, shrugging. "It needs more relish, too."

Phoebe shook her head. "That's not what I meant. I think I tasted *meat* in it. It's supposed to be a *veggie* burger!"

"No way," I told her. "There is no meat in this."

"Let me taste," Elise said, reaching over. She bit into the burger. "Mmm, yummy!"

"Wait, I want to try." Summer grabbed the burger from Elise and took a huge bite. She chewed thoughtfully. "I think they put pineapple in it!"

"Pineapple? Really?" I asked. "Let me taste it again." Summer handed me the burger, and I took another bite.

"Uh, guys? Can I have my lunch back?" Phoebe asked.

I handed Phoebe the bite of burger that was left. "Sorry, Phoebe. Looks like we got a little carried away."

Phoebe sighed. "That's okay. But I could have sworn I tasted meat in there."

I jumped up. "I'll order you fries," I said.

I hurried toward the counter to find the waitress. Sitting there on the last stool was Ms. Clare. My stomach sank when I saw who was right beside her. Dana Woletsky!

And I had a feeling I knew what they were talking about.

I ducked into the phone area around the corner. Luckily, they hadn't seen me.

My heart pounded hard. Was it possible? Had Dana reached a new all-time low? Was she actually trying to have me sent home?

DANA'S HIGHS + LOWS

"Are you sure about this, Dana?" I heard Ms. Clare ask.

"It's true. Back in Hilo Ashley Burke had a big party in her hotel room," Dana said.

I gasped. She *was* ratting on me!

"She ran up a huge room-service bill," Dana went on. "Then she had to make a secret deal with the manager of the hotel to pay it off."

I clamped a hand over my mouth. I was doomed. I had to do some damage control—fast!

I ran back to the counter.

Ms. Clare raised her eyebrows. "Ashley, what a coincidence. Dana was just telling me about a little party you had. Would you like to explain?" she asked.

I glanced at Dana. She looked totally smug.

"Well, I *did* have a party," I said. "I guess Summer and Elise and I were so bummed about not being in Wild Hawaii that we wanted to cheer ourselves up."

Okay, so that wasn't exactly true. We were happy to be kicked out of Wild Hawaii. But Ms. Clare didn't have to know that.

"We found out later that the room service wasn't included in our vacation," I went on. "We didn't have the money to pay for what we ordered so we went to the manager and offered to work it off." I looked at the floor. "We were afraid to tell you."

Ms. Clare folded her arms. "Ashley, you should have come to me when it happened," she said. "That would have been the right thing to do."

"I know," I replied. "And I'm really sorry. But we were too embarrassed. We waited on tables and washed dishes and cleaned rooms for days."

Ms. Clare was silent for a minute. Was she going to send me home? I held my breath.

Finally our chaperone smiled and patted my shoulder. "I think you've learned your lesson," she said. "But from now on, no more room service, okay?"

I let out a huge sigh of relief. "Thank you, Ms. Clare!" I exclaimed. "I'll be on my best behavior for the rest of the trip."

Ms. Clare nodded and turned back to her lunch.

I smiled at Dana, who scowled and stomped off.

Yes! I cheered. Now I could relax and enjoy this awesome vacation!

Dear Diary,

I caught Ashley up on Plan B of Operation: Autograph while we were at the pool this afternoon.

"What does this guy look like again?" Ashley asked.

I took a sip of my pineapple smoothie. "Ashley, how can you be so clueless about one of the most famous baseball players in the world?"

Ashley shrugged. "It's kind of like the time I was talking about clogs and you thought I meant the kind that stop up the drain."

I grinned. "Okay, never mind," I said. "Jake is six two with short black hair and tanned skin. He usually wears a red baseball cap—"

"Sounds like you're describing that guy over there," Ashley broke in.

I followed Ashley's gaze and almost dropped my smoothie. "That's him!"

Jake was settling into a beach chair across the deck. He slipped on a pair of sunglasses and started to read a magazine.

"He's alone. I've got to talk to him," I said. I jumped up from my chair—just as one of his bodyguards walked over and sat down next to him.

I froze in my tracks. "Oh, great." I groaned. "*Now* what do I do?"

"I know!" Ashley snapped her fingers. "You could pretend to be a towel girl and bring Jake some towels. The bodyguard won't stop you if he thinks you're just doing your job."

"Ashley, you are a genius!" I cried.

"You should bring him some sunscreen, too," Ashley suggested.

I nodded. "Jake always uses Sportsun, SPF 15. He even did a commercial for the stuff."

"Go for it!" Ashley cheered.

I ran to the towel hut and grabbed some fresh towels and a bottle of sunscreen. Then I put on my shades and pulled my hair into a ponytail. I didn't want his bodyguard to recognize me from yesterday.

"Wish me luck!" I said to Ashley over my shoulder as I started toward Jake.

She gave me a thumbs-up sign.

I strolled over to Jake's chair. He glanced up and smiled.

"Can I offer you a fresh towel?" I asked. "I also have some Sportsun SPF 15 handy, just in case you need it."

Jake sat up in his chair. "Well, thanks," he said.

Yes! I thought. This was going great. "So, Jake, I was wondering—"

"Thanks, miss." Jake's bodyguard got out of his chair. He grabbed the towels and the sunscreen. "Mr. Nakamoto needs some privacy now."

"It's okay," Jake said to the bodyguard. "What were you going to say?" he asked me.

Ring, ring!

"Excuse me a second," Jake said. He pulled a cell phone out of his pocket and flipped it open. "Hello?"

"So was there anything else you wanted to ask

Mr. Nakamoto?" the bodyguard asked.

My heart started thudding in my chest. *Just tell him you want Jake to sign a napkin*, I thought. But I was so nervous! I mean, I knew the bodyguard wasn't going to let me stick around for an autograph. "Uh, I wanted to see if he needed a smoothie or something."

"He's all set," the guard replied. "He has a smoothie right here." He pointed to a cup resting on a small table next to Jake's chair.

I racked my brain for some other excuse to hang around.

"What do you mean, the deadline's been moved up?" Jake said into the phone.

"You should probably go now," the bodyguard told me. "Thanks."

I stared helplessly at Jake, but he didn't look like he was getting off the phone anytime soon. There was nothing I could do except leave.

I dragged myself back to my chair. Ashley leaned in. "So? How did it go?" she asked.

"Strike two," I replied.

Ashley looked puzzled. "Huh?"

"That's baseball talk for: I

didn't get the autograph this time, either," I explained glumly.

"Oh. Right," Ashley replied. "Does that mean one more strike and you're out?"

I hoped not.

Chapter 4

Monday

Dear Diary,

Okay, now I've moved on to Plan C of Operation: Autograph. I'm going to find out Jake's room number, stand outside his door, and ambush him when he comes out!

I asked for Jake's room number at the front desk, but they wouldn't tell me. So right after Ms. Clare and Mr. Turnbull took us on a glass-bottom boat ride, I walked into the hotel florist. I had an awesome idea.

"May I help you?" the man behind the counter asked.

"I'd like to have a rose delivered to a guest in the resort right away," I said.

The florist nodded. "Very well. What color?"

"Um, whatever," I said.

The man gave me a puzzled look. "And whom would you like it delivered to?" he asked.

"Jake Nakamoto," I replied.

"What would you like the card to say?" the man asked.

"Card?" I repeated blankly. "Um, I don't need a card."

The florist raised an eyebrow. "One rose, any color, for Jake Nakamoto," he said. "No card."

"Yup. Thanks!" I said. I paid the bill and walked out.

But I didn't go very far. I hung out in the hallway outside the florist's shop and watched as he boxed up a single pink rose and handed it to a delivery guy.

The guy nodded at something the florist said, then walked out of the store with the box.

Excellent! My plan was working.

The guy was going to deliver that rose to Jake's room. And when he did, I would be right behind him!

We both took the elevator to the top floor of the resort and got out. I made sure I stayed far enough behind the delivery guy so he wouldn't notice me. He walked to the end of the hall and knocked on a door that said Penthouse A. "Flower delivery for Mr. Nakamoto," he called.

The door opened and one of Jake's bodyguards stepped out. As he signed for the flower, a white, furry cat slipped out into the hall and ran toward me.

Snowball!

I grabbed the cat as she hurried

by me. No one even noticed. The bodyguard closed the door, and the delivery guy stepped back into the elevator.

"Purr-fect!" I told Snowball. "The bodyguards will be so grateful I brought you back, they'll have to let me talk to Jake."

Snowball hissed and twisted and jumped out of my arms.

"Snowball, come back!" I begged. "You're my best hope!"

I tried to grab the cat again, but she scurried down the hall.

"Snowball!" I whispered. "Come on, pleeease! Come to Mary-Kate!"

I inched closer and reached out my arms. The cat's green eyes squinted at me.

"Gotcha!" I cried, grabbing her.

I held the cat close to my chest so she couldn't get away.

"Mrwow!" Snowball wriggled back and forth.

"Good kitty, gooood kitty," I said as I speed-walked to Jake's room. I knocked on the door with my elbow. It wasn't easy. Snowball was squirming like crazy.

Okay, this is it, I thought. I was finally going to get to talk to Jake about the autograph!

Suddenly Snowball dug her claws into my arm. "Ow!" I cried.

I loosened my grip, and she jumped to the ground. One second later Jake's bodyguard opened the door.

Snowball ran straight into Jake's room. The

guard barely looked at me before he closed the door.

"Hey, wait a second!" I protested just as the door slammed in my face.

Strike three.

Dear Diary,

After a huge, delicious buffet dinner, Summer, Elise, and I decided to take a walk on the beach.

Phoebe wasn't feeling too well. I guess she was still recovering from her non-veggie burger.

And Mary-Kate was just too bummed to come with us. I feel really bad for her. She's been trying so hard to get that autograph for Campbell. I wish Campbell could see that Mary-Kate really is a great friend.

"Just look at that sky!" Summer breathed, tilting her head back.

I gazed up at the swirls of pink, purple, and blue

that painted the air. "It's beautiful," I agreed.

Then something weird happened. Some of the colors started blinking! Red, green, yellow . . . What was going on?

The lights got lower and lower until they were flashing just above the palm trees.

"That's really strange," I told my friends.

"They look just like those lights from the UFO in that movie we watched," Elise said slowly.

Summer gasped. "The killer pod people are returning," she cried. "It's really happening!"

"Get real, Summer," I said. "There's no such thing as—"

Summer and Elise started running down the beach toward the lights.

"Come on, Ashley!" Summer yelled. "We have to see where they went!"

We do? I thought, taking off after my friends. I had to admit, I was a little curious. We ran all the way to the other side of the resort.

"We lost them!" Summer cried when we reached a rose garden. She sounded really disappointed. "Where did the lights go?"

"It seemed like they were coming from right here," Elise said.

A bush rustled nearby.

Elise and Summer grabbed each other's arm in fright.

"Who's there?" I asked, a little nervous.

I inched toward the bush. "Hello?" I asked, pushing some leaves aside. I saw a lock of long, curly brown hair—Phoebe's hair.

"Guys, relax," I told Summer and Elise. "It's just Phoebe."

But why was she hiding in the bushes? And why wasn't she answering me? I tapped her on the shoulder. "Phoebe? You okay?"

Phoebe gasped. When she saw that it was me, she seemed to relax a little. "Oh . . . hi," she said. "Um, what's up?"

"Maybe I should ask *you* that," I replied. "What are you doing hiding in the rosebushes?"

"Oh . . . um . . . I'm not hiding. I just wanted to . . . get a closer look at this type of flower." She emerged from the bushes, holding her video camera and backpack. "They're pretty, right?"

"Sure," I said. Then I noticed the scratches. Red X marks covered both her arms. "Phoebe, you're bleeding. Look!"

"Oh . . . yeah," she said, not really concerned.

"From the thorns on the roses, I guess. I'm okay."

Summer and Elise ran up to her.

"Did you just see the UFO?" Summer demanded. "We saw the lights from the other side of the resort."

"UFO?" Phoebe repeated. She laughed nervously. "Uh, nope. No UFOs around here!"

"See, I told you," I said to Summer and Elise. But something weird was going on with Phoebe. She seemed so . . . distracted. I mean, how could she not notice those scratches?

"Whatever," Summer replied. She didn't look convinced, though.

"What are you taping?" I asked Phoebe. I peeked at the little screen on the video camera. "And I thought you said you were sick."

Phoebe quickly pulled the camera away from me. "This video is top secret!" she said. "No one can see it but me." She stuffed the camera into her backpack.

Whoa! I thought. "Sorry," I said. "I didn't mean to—"

"Look, I have to go," Phoebe said, standing up. "I'll see you guys later, okay? Bye." She took off back toward the beach.

"Hmmm. Was Phoebe acting really strange just

now or what?" I asked Summer and Elise.

"Totally weird," Summer replied. "And I bet I know why."

She picked up a small blue metal tube from the ground. "This fell out of Phoebe's backpack when she put the camera in it."

"What is it?" Elise asked.

I peered closer. "I bet that's just a broken pen or something."

"That *National Inquisitor* article said that they found scraps of blue metal just like this at the scene of the other alien sighting," Summer pointed out. "They think it was part of the spaceship."

Elise gasped. "No way!"

"There's only one explanation," Summer continued. "A UFO was here. And Phoebe saw it!"

Chapter 5

Tuesday

Dear Diary,

Tonight we had a luau on the beach.
That's a special kind of Hawaiian bar-
becue where you roast a pig over an
open fire, which is dug into the ground.

We're talking about a whole pig with an apple in
its mouth!

Jeremy and Grant were crawling around the
beach on all fours and squealing, "Oink, oink!" I
swear, they are such babies!
Luckily, Ms. Clare made
them stop.

Campbell was sitting
with Julia, of course. They
were eating fresh pineapple
slices and giggling about something.

I sat across the fire from them, feeling pretty
awful. I still hadn't gotten Jake's autograph, and
Campbell wasn't showing any signs of coming
around.

Ashley sat down next to me and handed me a
coconut shell cup filled with mango juice. "So how
is Operation: Autograph going?" she asked.

I told Ashley all about the Snowball episode. "I

have no idea what to do next." I sighed. "I haven't spotted Jake all day. And Campbell is still ignoring me."

"Well, you've done all you could to make up with her," Ashley said. "Maybe you should just forget about the whole autograph thing and enjoy yourself."

"But she's my best friend, Ashley. What would you do if Phoebe all of a sudden hated you? Wouldn't you try everything to get her to *stop* hating you?"

"Okay, okay," Ashley said. "You've got a point." She paused. "You know what, Mary-Kate? Maybe you could show Campbell you're sorry by doing something nice for her. Not something huge, like getting Jake's autograph. Something small. Why don't you send over her favorite ice cream?"

"Well, I'll try it," I said. "But I'm still going to get that autograph if it's the last thing I do." I waved to a nearby waiter. He smiled and came over.

"Can you please send that girl with the blue T-shirt a bowl of chocolate fudge ice cream?" I pointed across the bonfire at Campbell.

"No problem, miss," the waiter said.

"Just make sure she knows it's from me, okay?" I added.

The waiter nodded. As he turned to leave, he almost crashed into Phoebe, who was running by.

"*There* she is!" Ashley said, jumping up. "I have to go catch Phoebe. She's been acting kind of weird lately."

"What's wrong with her?" I asked.

"I have no clue," Ashley answered. "But I'm going to find out!" She tore off after Phoebe.

I watched as the waiter came back with the ice cream and handed it to Campbell. He said something and pointed to me. Campbell shook her head and said something back to the waiter. He hesitated, then walked over to me.

"I'm sorry, miss. She says she doesn't want it," he told me. "Would you like to eat it instead?"

"No, thanks," I replied. I felt totally embarrassed. And now I was a little angry, too.

I'd tried and tried to make up with Campbell. But she obviously didn't care whether we'd ever be best friends again.

Well, if that's the way she wants it, I thought. *Then that's fine with me.*

From now on I was going to forget about trying to win back Campbell!

Two of a Kind Diaries

Dear Diary,

I am really getting worried about Phoebe. I'm sure she didn't see a UFO, but something is definitely up.

I tried to talk to her after the luau tonight. I found her in one of the elaborate hotel gardens, looking through a big telescope.

"Hey, Phoebe," I said. I pointed to the stuffed backpack she had slung over a shoulder. "Going somewhere?" I joked.

Phoebe straightened up so fast that she almost bonked her head on the telescope. "Oh, um, hi, Ashley. I'm not going anywhere. Why would you think I was going somewhere?" she said really fast.

"It was just a joke," I replied. "Anyway, what are you looking at?" I asked, gesturing to the telescope.

"Just the stars," Phoebe replied.

"Phoebe, there are no stars yet," I pointed out. "It's still daylight."

Phoebe shifted nervously. She glanced at the telescope, then at me.

We didn't say anything for a couple of minutes. I couldn't help staring at the scratches on her arms.

Phoebe noticed. "Oh, don't worry about those. They don't hurt. Really."

I don't know why, Diary, but our conversation seemed very, very tense. I decided to break the ice with one of Phoebe's favorite subjects—poetry.

"So, there's a special Hawaiian poetry reading on the beach tonight," I said. "Do you want to go?"

I figured there was no way she would refuse. Phoebe loved poetry so much she even decorated her half of our dorm room with posters of famous poets!

Phoebe shook her head. "Sorry, but no, thanks. I don't feel like listening to poetry."

Phoebe was turning down a night of poetry? "Phoebe, are you sure nothing is bothering you?" I asked. "You've been acting kind of—"

But Phoebe wasn't listening. She was bending over the telescope. She gasped suddenly. "They're back! I have to get down there right now!"

I tried to look over her shoulder, but I couldn't see what she was talking about. "Who's back?" I asked.

"Nobody," Phoebe said. "I'll see you later, okay?"

"What's going on? Phoebe, wait!" I called after her. But she didn't stop.

I looked through the telescope. It was pointed at a restaurant in the rose garden. Workers were loading boxes off a truck and carrying them into the building. What was the big deal?

Help, Diary! My friend has definitely turned into a total space case!

Chapter 6

Wednesday

Dear Diary,

Six A.M. is way too early to be awake. But that's what time I was up this morning.

It was Ashley's fault, actually. She woke me up by talking in her sleep. Something about telescopes and colored lights.

And now I can't fall back to sleep. So here I am, looking at the surf and writing in you.

I stared out the window. It was so pretty outside. The sun was just coming up and the sky was streaked with pink and gold. Palm trees swayed in the breeze. A group of seagulls swooped through the air.

Then I spotted a tall man in a red baseball cap jogging on the beach. I rubbed my eyes. No way! It was Jake Nakamoto—and he was alone!

What should I do? I know I said I was going to forget about Campbell. But maybe, just maybe I overreacted. And here was Jake—right in front of me! It was too easy. I had to try to get his autograph.

I slipped on my sneakers, grabbed a pen and paper, and ran out of the room.

Three minutes later I was tearing down the beach. I could see Jake not that far ahead. He wasn't wearing any shoes, and he was jogging on the wet sand where the waves rolled onto the shore.

The morning air was damp and chilly, but I was already working up a sweat. I was sprinting at full speed, trying to catch up. But I couldn't. "Jake! Hey, Jake!" I yelled.

He didn't seem to hear me. He just kept jogging. I tried to keep going, too, but finally I had to give up. Jake was just too fast. I stopped and clutched my side, breathing hard.

Then I saw two other joggers stretching at the entrance to the beach. I could hear them laughing and talking.

Julia. And Campbell.

I felt a pang. Normally I would go over to Campbell and tell her how I tried to outrun Jake Nakamoto. But hey, she'd probably just ignore me again, right?

I just wish I didn't feel so lonely without her.

Surf, Sand, and Secrets

Dear Diary,

I decided that there had to be a log-ical explanation for Phoebe's weird behavior. I just didn't know what it was yet.

I hoped that after this morning's hula-dancing class on the beach, I'd have a clear mind and would be able to figure it out. Our instructor was this hunky guy named Konane.

"I am *not* getting in a grass skirt and waving my arms around," Jeremy complained.

"Hula dancing isn't just for women," Konane told him. "In fact, some of the greatest hula dancers in our country have been men."

"Yeah, Jeremy," Hans teased, shaking his hips back and forth. "You'd look sooo cute with flowers in your hair!"

Konane turned to Hans. "Why don't you go first?"

Hans scowled as Konane showed him a couple of steps.

I looked around to find Phoebe. She was sitting away from the group and drawing something in a notebook.

I leaned over to Elise, Summer, and Mary-Kate.

"Phoebe has been totally out of it the last two days," I whispered.

"What do you mean?" Mary-Kate asked, stifling a yawn. She had gotten up really early this morning for some reason.

I told Mary-Kate about what happened on Monday, when Summer and Elise thought they saw a UFO and we found Phoebe with a video camera instead. Then I told all three of them about Phoebe and the telescope.

Summer's eyes grew enormous. "I know what Phoebe was trying to find through the telescope!"

"What?" Elise, Mary-Kate, and I asked at the same time.

"The spaceship!" Summer said.

Here we go again, I thought.

"We have proof that Phoebe saw the UFO on Monday," Summer went on. "The piece of blue metal, remember?"

This alien stuff was really getting out of hand. "You mean the broken pen?" I asked.

Summer ignored me. "The aliens had no choice but to take over Phoebe's brain after she saw them. It's perfectly logical."

"Oh, right." Mary-Kate giggled. "That's perfectly logical."

"I'm serious!" Summer said. "I read about it on the AlienEncounters Web site. When your mind is taken over by aliens, you start acting jumpy and out of it and not like yourself."

If anyone's brain had been taken over, it was Summer's. On the other hand, she was always acting kind of spacey.

I glanced at Phoebe. She certainly wasn't acting like herself these days. But I was sure there was another reason. And I was going to find out what it was.

"I'll be right back, guys," I said. I walked over to Phoebe, who was now scribbling like mad in a notebook.

"Hey, Phoebe," I said, plopping down next to her huge backpack. "You're still carrying this around? What's in here?"

Phoebe's head shot up. "Why do you keep asking me that?" she said kind of nervously. "Anyway, what's up?"

"Oh, I just came over to say hi," I replied. I glanced at her open book. There were drawings of strange disk-shaped things all over the page. Things that looked just like . . . UFOs.

No. Not UFOs, I reminded myself. Boy, Summer and Elise must have really gotten to me.

Phoebe saw me peeking and slammed her book shut. "Excuse me," she mumbled, jumping to her feet. "I've got to go."

"But you haven't even had a chance to hula yet," I pointed out. "I thought you said you couldn't wait to hula dance."

"I don't care. I'm too busy right now," Phoebe said. "See you later." She gathered her stuff and hurried away.

I sighed and rejoined the others. As I waited for my turn to hula, I made a mental list of all the weird stuff going on with Phoebe lately:

First she freaked out over a veggie burger.

Then there were the strange lights.

Then we found Phoebe hiding in the bushes.

Then she didn't notice the scratches on her arms.

Then there was the telescope incident.

Then there was the huge backpack she's been carrying everywhere.

Then she said no to a poetry reading.

Then she skipped out on hula lessons, which she'd been really looking forward to.

And now she was drawing UFOs in her notebook—or whatever they were.

Wow, that was a lot of weird stuff. No wonder Elise and Summer thought Phoebe had been taken over by space creatures.

The question was: How was I ever going to bring "Alien Phoebe" back to earth?

Chapter 7

Thursday

Dear Diary,

Today I am going to find out for sure what's going on with Phoebe.

Summer and Elise are now officially alien-obsessed, and Mary-Kate is still chasing after Jake. So that means it's up to me.

Phoebe didn't show up at lunch. I ordered a take-out veggie burger for her and went straight to her room.

I knocked on the door. No answer.

I was about to turn away, when I heard papers shuffling inside the room.

I knocked again, louder this time. "Phoebe?" I called. "It's me, Ashley! Can I come in?"

"I'm really busy," Phoebe said through the door.

"But I need to talk to you!" I insisted. "It's important."

I heard Phoebe sigh. She unlocked the door and swung it open.

I gasped. Phoebe was dressed in white capri pants, white platform shoes, and a 4-You T-shirt. Totally *not* her style!

"What's the matter?" she asked.

"Those clothes," I said. "They're so . . . not you!"

Phoebe glanced over her shoulder. "Yeah, well, I'm kind of in the middle or something right now. Can we talk later?"

I stood there stunned. Phoebe wearing non-vintage clothes was almost too much for me to process.

"Okay, then," Phoebe said when I didn't answer. "Bye!" She took the veggie burger from me and closed the door.

That was so rude! Now I knew something was *really* wrong. Phoebe's, like, the sweetest person on the planet. In this galaxy, anyway.

I had to talk to Mary-Kate. Right *now*.

But I couldn't find my sister anywhere. Instead, I ran into Summer and Elise in the hotel lobby. I told them all about my encounter with Phoebe.

"See?" Summer exclaimed. "Her mind has definitely been taken over by aliens. The new clothes are even more proof!"

That idea was so dumb, it wasn't even worth arguing about. But I didn't have any other explanation for the new Phoebe.

"Come on," Summer said. She grabbed my hand and Elise's hand, too. "I want to show you something."

Summer dragged us over to one of the hotel computers in the Internet Cafe. She logged on and punched in a Web address.

The screen turned black. Then a weird creature popped onto the screen. It had one eye in the center of its huge forehead like an octopus and an antenna sticking out of its head.

"This is the AlienEncounters Web site I told you about," Summer explained.

A menu popped up. Summer pointed to the last item on the menu. It said: HAS A LOVED ONE'S MIND BEEN TAKEN OVER BY ALIENS? CLICK HERE.

"That's what we want," she said excitedly and clicked on the text. A new Web page popped up on the screen.

"Look!" Summer said. "It says here that the first sign that someone's mind has been taken over by aliens is when 'the person displays uncharacteristic or unusual behavior.'"

"The new clothes!" Elise cried.

"Among other things," I added glumly.

"'Two. He/she avoids contact with friends and family,'" Summer read aloud.

"Phoebe's been avoiding me for days." I sighed.

"'Three. He/she acts nervous, vague, or skittish.'"

I groaned. "Go on."

"'Four,'" Summer said. "'He/she becomes obsessed with the night sky, stargazing, and other similar activities.'"

"The telescope," Elise pointed out.

I looked away from the computer screen. It was true. The Web site described Phoebe perfectly. But aliens weren't real. It couldn't be possible.

"*Now* do you believe me?" Summer asked.

Like I said, there was no use arguing with Summer. She was just too far gone on the whole alien question. But I had to get back to the point. Phoebe needed our help.

"Say I did believe you—and I'm not saying I do," I told Summer. "What could we do for her?"

Summer scrolled down the page on the computer. "Here it is. A section about how to help someone whose mind has been taken over by aliens," she reported.

"'The person has to wear a special metal hat and stand in front of a big mirror,'" Elise read over Summer's shoulder. She frowned. "What's that supposed to do?"

"Duh. The metal blocks the alien transmissions to Phoebe's brain," Summer said. "And then you have to chant a bunch of special words," she added. "I'll print them out for you."

"We have to do this, Ashley," Elise said urgently. "We have to bring Phoebe back to us!"

This was all too bizarre. "Um, guys," I began. "I don't think—"

"You should do it, Ashley," Elise broke in. "You're Phoebe's roommate. You know her best. She trusts you."

Summer handed me the printout. "May the Force be with you," she said.

I can't believe this, I thought. But I had to try *something.* At this point the anti-brainwashing plan was beginning to look good.

Dear Diary,

Has everyone on this trip gone crazy?

It's bad enough that Campbell will probably never speak to me again. But now some of our friends are insisting there are aliens here in Hawaii.

At first the whole idea was kind of funny. But now it's getting serious.

Ashley just told me that Summer and Elise want her to get Phoebe to wear some weird hat and stand in front of a mirror, because Phoebe's mind has been taken over by aliens.

Ashley thinks that's pretty crazy. But she figures it's an excuse to try and reach Phoebe again.

I guess I must be going crazy, too. Because Ashley just asked me to help her do it—and I said yes!

Chapter 8

Thursday

Dear Diary,

I took the night off from Operation: Autograph to help Ashley with Operation: Save Phoebe from Aliens.  Jake didn't seem to be around the hotel much anyway. It seemed almost as if he'd disappeared. Maybe he's just trying to avoid autograph-hungry fans (like me).

Or *maybe* he was abducted by those aliens. (Ha-ha!)

Ashley and I sat on my bed and tried to brainstorm the perfect plan. I'm a real pro at plans now.

"Okay, so we have to get Phoebe to wear a metal hat and stand in front of a mirror," Ashley explained.

I leaned back on my pillow. "Sounds like we're going to have to trick her."

"Hmmm," Ashley said, tapping a finger against her lip. "Phoebe isn't easy to trick. She's so logical. Well, usually."

"I know!" I cried. "You said she's into trendy clothes these days, right?"

Ashley shrugged. "So?"

"So we'll make a special hat for her as a present and tell her it's the cool thing to wear. You know, to go with her new look."

"Okay," Ashley said slowly. "But then we'll all need hats!"

I nodded. "No problem. We'll make Phoebe try hers on in front of the bathroom mirror. And while she's standing there, you can try to talk to her again."

"That's totally brilliant!" Ashley exclaimed.

"Thanks," I said. "Let's just hope it's brilliant enough to work."

"Um, Mary-Kate?" Ashley asked. "There's just one thing."

"What's that?" I said.

"Where do we get metal hats?"

I sighed. It's hard to be brilliant *all* the time. But I'd come up with something to help Ashley.

And Alien Phoebe.

Dear Diary,

So there we were, standing in front of Phoebe's door the next morning. But Mary-Kate wasn't the only one with me. Summer and Elise decided to join us.

"We had to come," Summer said. "What if the

63

aliens showed up? You would totally need our help."

"All right," I replied. "But don't say anything. I want to do all the talking." I didn't want Summer saying anything about aliens to Phoebe.

We all looked pretty weird, wearing those metal hats. We'd made them out of baseball caps, aluminum foil, wire, and old soda cans. But we had to wear them if this plan was going to work.

"This is going to be sooo exciting," Summer said.

"Let's just hope it works," I muttered. "Or we may lose Phoebe for good."

Mary-Kate gave me a thumbs-up. "All systems are go," she said.

I took a deep breath and knocked on Phoebe's door again.

"Who is it?" Phoebe called.

"It's Ashley and Mary-Kate," I said. "And Summer and Elise."

The door opened. This time Phoebe was dressed in denim shorts, a black T-shirt with a blue rhinestone star on it, and a brand-new pair of platform sneakers.

I plastered a huge smile on my face. "Hi, Phoebe! Guess what? We brought you a present." I held out the extra hat we'd made.

Phoebe glanced at me and then at the rest of us.

"That's really nice, guys," she said. "Could you give it to me later?" She started to close the door.

Mary-Kate stepped in front of me and stuck her foot in the door. "But we really want you to have it now," she said sweetly. "It's the latest fashion thing. You know, a fad. It could go out of style before you wear it."

Phoebe hesitated. Then she opened the door wider and let us in. "Okay. But you can only hang out for a second."

We all quickly walked into the room. A bunch of notebooks were spread out on Phoebe's bed. She quickly scooped them up and shoved them into a drawer.

Mary-Kate and I exchanged a look. I knew we were wondering the same thing. What was in those notebooks?

Phoebe stuffed her hands into her pockets. "So what did you bring me?" she asked.

Summer grabbed the hat from me and placed it on Phoebe's head. "Ta-da!" she said brightly.

"Uh . . . what's this?" Phoebe asked.

"The latest in Hawaiian headwear!" I replied. "You know, to go with your, um, new look."

"Well, okay." Phoebe shrugged. "Thanks."

"You've got to see how great it looks!" Mary-

Kate insisted. She started pushing Phoebe toward the bathroom. The entire wall above the sink was covered with a mirror. Summer reached into her beach bag and whipped out a piece of paper.

"Mirabilis yokum sageonis filatis. Mirabilis yokum sageonis filatis . . ." Summer began.

Elise joined in.

I groaned. This was exactly why I didn't want Summer to speak! How was I supposed to get Phoebe to listen to me now?

Phoebe turned and stared at me in total confusion. "Ashley, what's going on?"

"It's a special good-luck chant for your new hat!" Mary-Kate improvised.

"Mirabilis yokum sageonis filatis. Mirabilis yokum sageonis filatis . . ." Summer and Elise kept chanting.

Phoebe shook her head. "You guys are acting really weird," she said. "You're starting to freak me out!"

Mary-Kate motioned for me to hurry up. "Um, look, Phoebe, we have to talk to you," I said quickly. "It's for your own good."

Phoebe yanked off the hat. "Look, I don't know what's going on here," she said, "but I have important things to do. I'm on a deadline."

"We had to do all this stuff," Mary-Kate said. "We couldn't reach you any other way."

"Reach me?" Phoebe demanded. "What are you talking about?"

"Your mind has been taken over by aliens!" Summer blurted out.

Phoebe gaped at all of us. "What?" she said.

"Well, that's just it, Phoebe," I began. "Some people think"—I glanced at Summer and Elise— "that aliens may have taken over your brain. But—"

Phoebe whirled around again so fast that the hat slid off her head. Summer and Elise stopped chanting.

"Are you all nuts?" she cried.

"Not me!" I said quickly. "This whole thing was Summer's idea. And even though I don't believe—"

"I really don't have time for this," Phoebe said. "Everybody out!" She started pushing all four of us toward the door. "Go chase some spaceships or something."

"Denial," Summer said to me under her breath. "It's another one of the signs."

"I'll talk to you later, after you've gotten your

own brains back," Phoebe said. "And after I finish what I'm working on."

Before the door slammed behind us, I looked over Phoebe's shoulder. Her computer screen was glowing green in the darkened room. And there was a half-eaten veggie burger on her desk.

For some reason I got a chill. What was Phoebe doing? What could be so important?

"Good-bye," Phoebe called through the door. "And have a nice trip to Mars."

The four of us started slowly back down the hall, feeling totally discouraged. And that's when we saw it.

 A trail of tiny purple shells . . .

Chapter 9

Friday

Dear Diary,

It's almost bedtime. I'm sitting on the terrace outside our hotel room. Ashley is watching the Sci Fi Channel with Summer and Elise. Sort of.

They're all still bummed about the Phoebe situation. Summer and Elise are trying to figure out the deal with the trail of shells.

I keep telling them that those shells are all over the resort, but they keep insisting that the aliens put them there.

Ashley was right. No more space movies for them!

I really wish I could help Ashley brainstorm a way to deal with Phoebe. But I have my own thinking to do. Did I really want to come up with another plan to get Jake's autograph for Campbell? Even though I was angry with her, the answer was yes.

Watching the waves and the palm trees helps me think. Oh, and the caramel-swirl ice cream cone I got downstairs helps, too.

I'm thinking.

I'm still thinking.

Ugh! I can't come up with anything!

I feel so helpless. I have to admit I really miss Campbell. If she never talks to me again, who am I going to sneak out of the dorm with late at night to grab a slice of pizza from the kitchen? Who am I going to talk about baseball with? And who else but Campbell would want to spend an entire Saturday at the movie theater with me watching four movies in a row?

I guess those fun times are over. I'll probably have to get a new roommate next fall, too.

I know it's not like me to give up. But after all this, I don't know what else to do. I've tried everything!

It's sad, but I just have to face it. Campbell and I will never be friends again.

Dear Diary,

You'll never guess what happened. 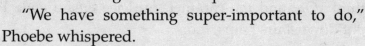 Phoebe ran up and grabbed me by the arm right after wave-running class. She was wearing a Hawaiian-print mini dress.

"We have something super-important to do," Phoebe whispered.

"Can I change into my clothes first?" I asked, pointing to the bathing suit I was wearing.

Phoebe shook her head. "There's no time."

"Okay," I said. Was this about what Phoebe had been working on?

"In an hour the hotel's rose garden restaurant starts serving lunch," Phoebe explained. "If we sneak into the kitchen now, we can catch them!"

"Catch who?" I asked. I was really beginning to worry now. And why were we going to the rose garden? "Phoebe, does this have anything to do with"—I couldn't believe I was about to say it—"aliens?"

"There's no time to explain the whole thing now," Phoebe said. "But the story is out of this world. It's so huge I might even sell it to a real newspaper!" Phoebe reached into her backpack and whipped out her video camera. "We're going to get the whole thing on tape."

A story about aliens . . . in a kitchen? Ooookay. I decided just to play along. Anything to help my roommate—and find out once and for all what was going on.

We sneaked down the hall to the kitchen and peeked inside.

The kitchen was crawling with men and women in checkered pants who were chopping vegetables and washing pots and pans.

"How are we going to get in there without anyone seeing us?" I whispered.

Phoebe held up her hand. "I have a plan. Just wait."

We waited and waited. Then all of a sudden Phoebe whispered, "Now! We're going in!"

She opened the doors, ducked down, and raced toward a chopping table that had a dust ruffle hanging over the sides. I ran in behind her, and we both dropped under the table.

My heart was racing. I took a few deep breaths and tried to calm down. "Now what?" I whispered. "What, um . . . are we looking for?"

"Now we wait," Phoebe replied, turning on the video camera.

This was making me a little nervous. What if Ms. Clare found out I was staking out the kitchen in search of little green men? She'd send me home for sure!

I leaned back on the floor. "Ewww!" I cried softly  as my hand touched something squishy. It was an ancient-looking onion ring.

ANCIENT-
LOOKING
ONION
RING

"Oh, gross," I said, wiping my hand against my bathing suit.

All of a sudden the kitchen doors swung open. A

man wearing a tall white chef's hat walked in. Another man was right behind him.

"Now, about that burger recipe," the chef said to the man.

I took a look at the man's face. My eyes widened in surprise.

"Hey!" I whispered. "That's Jake Nakamoto, the famous baseball player."

"What's he doing in here?" Phoebe wondered.

"I've been thinking about it," Jake replied, "and I think we should add even more meat to the veggie burgers."

I was totally confused. "Why would Jake tell the chef to put meat in the veggie burgers?" I whispered.

Phoebe shrugged. "I have no idea," she said. "But with luck we're about to find out."

"I have a conference call in five minutes," Jake went on. "Why don't we finish discussing this later?"

"Very good, sir," the chef replied.

Jake said good-bye and left.

"This is big," Phoebe muttered. "This is really big!" She yanked on my hand. "Let's go!"

"Where are we going now?" I asked.

"Duh!" Phoebe announced. "We're going to follow Jake!"

Chapter 10

Saturday

Dear Diary,

Phoebe and I rushed out of the 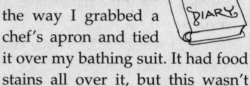 kitchen. Along the way I grabbed a chef's apron and tied it over my bathing suit. It had food stains all over it, but this wasn't exactly the time to be picky.

We could see Jake hurrying down the hall. He was wearing his shades, and he had his baseball cap low over his forehead.

Wait until Mary-Kate hears about this! I thought.

"I can't believe Jake Nakamoto is involved in this scam," Phoebe said.

"Scam?" I asked blankly.

But Phoebe was pulling me along at warp speed. "There he goes!" she cried.

Jake turned down the hall and disappeared from view.

Phoebe held up her video camera. "We have to stay with him," she insisted.

"Uh, Phoebe, is Jake an . . . alien?" I asked. Is that what Phoebe was thinking? Was she filming a segment for some TV unreality show?

Phoebe didn't answer. We were both running too fast after Jake. We passed Elise and Summer coming out of one of the gift shops. They were carrying a bunch of magazines.

"Ashley, where are you going?" Elise asked.

"And what are you *wearing*?" Summer cried. "Gross."

"No time now. Talk to you later!" I called.

"We'd better make a new hat for Ashley, too," I heard Elise say as I raced by.

We turned the corner. Jake was only about ten feet down the hall.

"Jake, stop!" Phoebe yelled.

Jake turned around. He glanced at Phoebe's video camera, then hurried to the elevator bank and pressed the button about ten times.

Phoebe and I sprinted like crazy to catch up. We were almost there when the elevator doors opened. "Sorry, girls. No time for autographs right now," Jake said as he stepped in.

"Wait, Mr. Nakamoto!" Phoebe said. "We need to talk to you. Take us with you."

I looked at Phoebe in alarm. "Take us where?" I said.

But just then the elevator doors closed in our faces.

"Oh, man!" Phoebe said, leaning back against the wall. "We just blew our big chance."

Our big chance for what? A ride in an alien spaceship?

Poor Phoebe was in worse shape than I thought.

Dear Diary,

You will never, ever believe what happened to me today. I was in the elevator going to my room when the doors opened and a man jumped in.

 "That was close," he muttered and pressed Penthouse.

My mouth dropped open. I blinked a few times to make sure I wasn't seeing things.

Standing next to me, without a single bodyguard, was Jake Nakamoto!

I took a deep breath. "H-hi," I said.

Jake nodded at me. "Hi."

Jake Nakamoto just said hi to me! I silently screamed. *Okay, Mary-Kate, get a grip.*

"Um, I think you're a great baseball player," I went on.

Jake smiled. "Well, thanks."

"That was an awesome grand slam you hit in Game Three of the playoffs last year," I told him.

"Yeah, that was one of my favorites, too," Jake said. "Wish I'd hit another one this season."

I can't believe we're having a real conversation, I said to myself. Now was the perfect time to ask him for an autograph.

"Jake, can you please do me a really big favor?" I said.

Jake raised an eyebrow. "What's that?" he replied.

"My best friend—well, my ex best friend—is your number one fan," I explained. "Even bigger than me. She actually knows all your batting averages from the time you started out in the minor leagues."

"Really?" Jake said. He sounded surprised. And a little flattered, I think.

"Well, Campbell—that's my friend's name—she and I had a big fight," I went on. "It was all my fault, and now she won't speak to me. But if I got your autograph for her, I'm sure she'd forgive me."

The elevator doors opened at the top floor. He stepped out.

Oh, no! I thought. *Is it happening again? Is he just going to disappear?*

Jake turned back and held open the door. "Okay," he said. "I'll give you an autograph for your friend. But let's keep it just between us, okay?"

"Oh, thank you, thank you, Jake!" I gushed, reaching into my pocket for a pen and paper.

Oh, no. I left them in my room! "Uh, do you have any paper?" I asked hopefully.

Jake shook his head. "Listen, I'm really late for a conference call," he said. "But I'll tell you what. Why don't you meet me at Diamond Point tomorrow morning—say, six A.M.—and I'll give you that autograph?"

Six? Ugh. But hey, at this point I'd get up at three! I nodded eagerly.

"I know that's kind of early, but my morning jog is the only time I have to myself. And don't worry, one of my bodyguards does keep a watch on the beach with binoculars, so you'll be safe."

"No problem," I said. " I'll be there!"

How about that, Diary? All I needed was one tiny miracle. And I finally got it!

Chapter 11

Sunday

Dear Diary,

This journalism stuff is hard work. Phoebe and I woke up at six this morning. Mary-Kate told me that she saw Jake jogging by himself early the other day so I thought, with any luck, we might catch him today.

Mary-Kate wasn't in her bed. She had left me a note that said "Went for a walk."

I feel as if I haven't seen Mary-Kate in forever. Phoebe and I were super-busy trying to track down Jake yesterday. But she still refuses to tell me exactly what's going on.

Either Phoebe thinks Jake is an alien or she thinks he's trying to meet up with aliens. She keeps muttering something about a "plan."

I haven't figured it out yet. But I'm going to stick really close to Phoebe so I can keep an eye on her.

"Ashley, open up!" Phoebe called from the hallway, pounding on the door.

I rolled out of bed to let her in. She was dressed in vintage clam-diggers and an old khaki shirt. Was "Normal Phoebe" back? Well, normal for *her*, anyway!

"Ready to go?" she asked.

"Uh-huh." I nodded. We walked down to the beach. The air was cool and salty-smelling. The

sand was damp and covered with broken shells and seaweed.

"Let's try this way," I suggested, pointing left. "That's the direction my sister said Jake ran the other day."

"Okay," Phoebe agreed. She pulled her video camera out of her backpack. "I'm all set."

We trudged along the beach for about a mile or so. Finally I saw a man wearing a baseball cap, jogging toward Diamond Point. Bingo!

"We've got him now!" Phoebe cried. "Let's go!"

Dear Diary,

How cool am I? I had a secret meeting with a famous baseball player this morning. Jake Nakamoto is the best!

"Hey," he called as he jogged over to me.

"Hi!" I said, smiling. "Thanks again for meeting me here."

"My pleasure." Jake leaned against a rock. "When you told me about your friend, I realized something. I've been so wrapped up in business lately, I've forgotten to take time out for the thing I love the most. Talking to my fans!"

"Well, I'm sure glad you took the time out to talk to me!" I exclaimed.

Jake grinned. "So what do you want me to sign?" I reached down to pull a piece of paper from my backpack. That's when I saw two girls running toward us like crazy.

Oh, no! I thought.

Then I looked closer. It was Ashley and Phoebe! *What are they doing here?* I wondered.

"Mr. Nakamoto!" Phoebe yelled. "We have a few questions for you!"

Jake shook his head. "You two again," he said. "You were chasing me yesterday. What do you want? Autographs?"

Phoebe pointed the video camera right at his face. "We're reporters," she said breathlessly. "What were you doing in the hotel kitchen yesterday morning?"

Ashley looked a little nervous. "Um, Phoebe," she said. "I don't think this is such a good idea."

"What are you talking about?" Jake asked.

"Don't deny it, mister. We know the truth." Phoebe zoomed the video camera lens closer to his face.

Jake held his hands up in front of his face. Then he turned to me with a frown. "Sorry, Mary-Kate. I can't do this right now. It's getting out of hand." He started running back toward the hotel.

"You can run if you want, Mr. Nakamoto!" Phoebe called after him. "But the truth will come out!"

Ashley put an arm around Phoebe's shoulders. "Phoebe, everything's going to be okay," she said. "Just take it easy, all right?"

Then she turned to me. "Mary-Kate, what are you doing here?" she asked.

"Me? What about *you*?" I dropped to the sand, totally bummed. "I was about to get Jake's autograph," I said miserably. "But you guys just blew it!"

Chapter 12

Monday

Dear Diary,

Mary-Kate was really mad at us yesterday for almost blowing her big chance with Jake.

Luckily, she ran after him and convinced him to come back.

"Okay, can someone please explain what is going on here?" Jake asked. "Why do you kids keep following me?"

"We were just trying to investigate the veggie-burger scam," Phoebe explained.

"Huh?" Jake looked totally confused.

I was confused, too. Even more than before. Veggie-burger scam?

"We know all about it, Mr. Nakamoto," Phoebe said. "How the hotel has been putting meat in the veggie burgers . . . because you told them to do it!"

To my surprise, instead of yelling at Phoebe, Jake burst out laughing. "That is so funny," Jake said. "A veggie-burger scam!"

Mary-Kate glared at me, then at Phoebe.

"Are you saying that you don't know anything about it?" Phoebe asked, putting her hands on her hips.

"Uh, no," Jake replied.

"Wait a minute. What *were* you doing in the rose garden restaurant's kitchen yesterday?" I asked.

"If you girls must know," Jake said, "I'm opening a sports restaurant here at the resort. I was going over the menu with the chef. He's going to start at my place as soon as it opens."

"So you *are* going to put meat in the veggie burgers," I said slowly. "But that's lying. It's false advertising."

"Not to mention totally gross," Phoebe put in.

"It's a brand-new recipe for a Nakamoto burger,"  Jake told us, throwing up his hands. "It's a veggie *hamburger*! It has meat *and* vegetables in it, which means less fat but great taste!"

Phoebe just stood there with her mouth hanging open. I felt really sorry for her. Her big story wasn't really a story at all. She probably felt totally stupid!

"A veggie hamburger. That an awesome idea!" Mary-Kate said eagerly. "When does your restaurant open? Can we go?"

"It's opening next month," Jake went on. "In fact, we had a huge outdoor photo shoot here last week

for the upcoming publicity campaign. We were trying to keep it top secret. But the crew used so many
bright, flashing lights that a bunch of hotel guests
turned up to see what was going on."

I gulped. "Bright lights?" I said. "That shoot
wasn't in the rose garden, was it?"

Jake nodded. "Yup."

That meant Elise and Summer's "UFO" was
really flashbulbs from Jake's photo shoot!

"I'd really appreciate it if you kept this information to yourselves for another week," Jake said. He
wagged his finger at Phoebe and me. "Especially
you two."

"I'll make sure they do," Mary-Kate chimed in.

Phoebe looked at me. "So much for my big
undercover story," she said. "I was planning to sell
it to *The Hawaii Journal*."

"Not *The National Inquisitor*?" I asked her.

Phoebe grinned. "That worthless waste of good
paper? Not if it was the last newspaper in the galaxy!"

Dear Diary,
I can't believe Phoebe thought Jake
was part of a veggie-burger scam. And
Ashley thought Phoebe thought Jake
was an alien!

When Phoebe told Jake her side of the story, he cracked up. And when Phoebe heard Ashley's story about her, she started rolling around the sand in hysterics. I couldn't help laughing, too.

But all's well that ends well.

Jake said that he still wanted to give me that autograph.

He wrote:

FOR MY NUMBER ONE FAN, CAMPBELL
WITH BEST WISHES,
JAKE NAKAMOTO

And then he wrote another one for *me*!

"Thanks, Jake!" I said as he handed it to me. Then I had a great idea. "Phoebe, can I borrow your video camera?" I asked.

"Sure," Phoebe said, handing it over.

I turned to Jake. "I know you've already done me a huge favor," I said. "But would you mind saying hello to Campbell on tape for me?"

Jake didn't even hesitate. "Sure, why not?"

I clicked on the camera. Jake posed in front of the rolling waves and the sunrise and began talking into the camera.

"Hey, Campbell! This is Jake Nakamoto. I heard

you're really into baseball. It's good to know there are fans like you out there, cheering me on. It helps me to play my best!

"I'm talking to you now because of someone who cares about you very much. It's your best friend, Mary-Kate. She feels really bad that the two of you have been fighting.

"It would mean a lot to me if you could give her a break. Because it would be a shame if the two of you weren't friends anymore.

"Anyway, keep hitting those home runs, Campbell! And thanks for being such a big fan!"

I clicked the camera off. "That was awesome!" I cried. I couldn't help it. I gave Jake a huge hug.

Jake smiled. "I hope everything works out."

"I know it will," I told him. And I meant it.

If this didn't win Campbell back, nothing would!

Chapter 13

Tuesday

Dear Diary,

This is our last night on Kauai. Tomorrow we're heading back to New Hampshire. From there we're all taking separate flights back to our hometowns. And then it will be Summer Vacation: Part Two in good old Chicago!

After I finished packing, I went to visit Phoebe in her room.

I knocked on her door.

"Come in!" Phoebe called.

I went inside. Phoebe was sitting at her desk,

 leafing through her notebook. Her suitcase and duffel bag were on the floor, all closed up. I noticed that her trendy outfits were sticking out of the waste-basket.

"You're not going to throw those out, are you?" I said in horror.

Phoebe shrugged. "You can have them if you want. They were just my disguises. I was trying to blend in with all the other hotel guests."

I rescued the clothes and tucked them under my

arm. "So what are you doing now? I'm really sorry you didn't get your big story."

Phoebe grinned. "Are you kidding me? I did!"

"What do you mean?" I asked.

"You don't think the story behind Jake Nakamoto's new restaurant is a good idea?" Phoebe asked. "For when it opens, I mean?"

"Hey, yeah," I said. "Sounds great!"

"And guess what he's going to call the restaurant?" Phoebe asked. "Planet Jake!"

The door burst open, and Summer and Elise rushed in. Summer was carrying two new metal hats. Elise was carrying a big makeup mirror.

Before Phoebe and I could react, Summer slipped the hats on both of us. Elise held up the mirror, then started chanting:

"Mirabilis yokum sageonis filatis. Mirabilis yokum sageonis filatis . . ."

Phoebe yanked off her hat and stood up. "You guys don't understand. Ashley and I are *fine!*"

"That's what the aliens want you to think," Elise told us.

I rolled my eyes. Even when they heard the truth,

Two of a Kind Diaries

I had a feeling Summer and Elise were still going to believe in aliens!

Dear Diary,

After dinner I went back to my room to grab Jake's autograph and video for Campbell. I was really nervous about giving them to her. What would she say?

Before I had a chance to do that, though, there was a knock at my door.

You'll never believe who it was, Diary. Campbell!

"Campbell?" I said, totally surprised. "What are you doing here?

"Please let me in, just for a second," she pleaded. "I have something I need to tell you."

I opened the door wider.

Campbell hesitated, then stepped into the room.

I took a deep breath and waited to hear what she had to say.

"I've been a real jerk, Mary-Kate," she burst out. "I was hurt, but I had no right to act that way. Can you ever forgive me?"

I stood there for a minute in total shock. Campbell was apologizing to me? I didn't know what to say.

"Well, I don't blame you for hating me,"

Campbell said. She headed for the door. "I'll just leave."

"No, wait," I said. "Campbell, of course I forgive you. But do you forgive me?"

"Are you kidding?" Campbell said. "I've missed you so much! I wanted to apologize sooner, but after the way I acted, I didn't think you'd ever talk to me again."

"Really?" I asked. "I missed you, too."

We gave each other a huge hug.

Then I took the autograph off my dresser and handed it to Campbell. "Here," I said. "I got this for you."

Campbell gasped when she saw what it was. "How?" she exclaimed. "Jake's bodyguards said he wasn't signing autographs!"

"Let's just say I tried really, really hard," I said with a grin.

Campbell broke into a smile. "Wow, thanks, Mary-Kate! That's so nice of you."

I decided it was time for Present Number Two. I reached into my backpack again and pulled out the videotape.

"I have something else for you," I said. I popped

the tape into the VCR, turned on the TV, and hit Play. Jake's face filled up the screen.

Campbell ran up to the screen to get a closer look.

When the tape was finished, I hit the stop button. Campbell looked a little stunned. Then she swiped at her eyes. "Th-th-this is amazing," she sputtered. "Only a really good friend—the best friend in the whole world—would do something like this!"

She reached over and hugged me again. I hugged her back.

"I'm so glad we're friends again!" Campbell cried.

"Me, too," I agreed. We slapped palms. I had my best bud back!

We ordered chocolate-fudge ice cream from room service—Campbell's treat—and watched Jake's video about forty-nine more times.

"It's too bad we have to say good-bye for the summer just when we made up," I said.

Campbell grinned. "Don't worry! We'll have a blast when we're roommates again in September."

"Count on it!" I told her.

I never thought I would say this, Diary, but I can't wait for school to start again!

Together
Again

#25 Closer Than Ever

"Ashley, we haven't hung out in forever!" Mary-Kate Burke complained to her sister. It was lunchtime at White Oak Academy, and Mary-Kate and her friends were hanging out in the dining hall.

"I know." Ashley put down her juice box. "I thought I'd see more of you in boarding school, not less. I'm really starting to miss you."

"I miss you, too!" Mary-Kate replied.

Mary-Kate's roommate, Campbell Smith, groaned. "Okay, enough warm and fuzzy," she said. "There's got to be a way for you to spend more time together."

"Hey, I know!" Mary-Kate cried. "What if Ashley and I became roommates for a week?"

"That's a great idea!" Ashley cheered.

"Phoebe and I can room together," Campbell suggested.

Phoebe Cahill, Ashley's roommate, nodded. "Sounds good to me," she said.

"Great," Mary-Kate said. "After we get permission, it's all systems go!"

"Speaking of going," Ashley said. She took one last bite of her sandwich and stood up. "I've got to run. See you guys later!"

Mary-Kate watched as Ashley left the dining room. "Roomies," she said. "I like the sound of that!"

"You know, Mary-Kate," Phoebe said, "I didn't want to say anything when Ashley was around, but rooming with your sister is not exactly easy."

"Why not?" Mary-Kate asked. "She was fine when we were roommates at home in Chicago."

"Well, Ashley has changed since she started White Oak," Phoebe explained. "Now she goes to bed super-early and our closet is so stuffed with her clothes it's about to explode!"

"There's still time to back out," Campbell said.

Mary-Kate stared at Campbell. "Why would I want to back out? I'm sure Ashley will be a great roommate."

"But what about her annoying habits?" Phoebe persisted.

Mary-Kate shrugged. "Whatever. I bet I can get

her to change those habits," she replied.

Phoebe and Campbell glanced at each other.

"Did you say . . . bet?" Campbell grinned.

"Yes." Mary-Kate raised her eyebrows. "Why?"

"Because we bet you can't change those habits," Phoebe said. "Loser has to do the winner's laundry for a whole month!"

"Stinky gym socks and all!" Campbell added.

Mary-Kate pictured Campbell's gym socks and gulped. They sure were stinky. But what did she care? This was one bet she was sure she would win!

Mary-Kate smiled. "Girls," she said, "you are on!"

Win a Mary-Kate and Ashley Fun in the Sun Gift Pack!

ENTER BELOW TO WIN EVERYTHING YOU NEED FOR A GREAT DAY AT THE BEACH!

- A portable stereo system
- Mary-Kate and Ashley Greatest Hits and Greatest Hits II music CDs
- An autographed Mary-Kate and Ashley summer reading library
- Mary-Kate and Ashley brand sunglasses, beach towel, beach ball and T-shirt
- Much, much more…

Mail to: **MARY-KATE AND ASHLEY FUN IN THE SUN GIFT PACK SWEEPSTAKES**
C/O HarperEntertainment
Attention: Children's Marketing Department
10 East 53rd Street, New York, NY 10022

No purchase necessary.

Name: _____

Address: _____

City: _____ State: _____ Zip: _____

Phone: _____ Age: _____

TWO OF A KIND™
Mary-Kate & Ashley Fun in the Sun Gift Pack Sweepstakes

OFFICIAL RULES:

1. No purchase necessary.

2. To enter complete the official entry form or hand print your name, address, age, and phone number along with the words "TWO OF A KIND Fun in the Sun Sweepstakes" on a 3" x 5" card and mail to: TWO OF A KIND Fun in the Sun Sweepstakes, c/o HarperEntertainment, Attn: Children's Marketing Department, 10 East 53rd Street, New York, NY 10022. Entries must be received **no later than October 31, 2002.** Enter as often as you wish, but each entry must be mailed separately. One entry per envelope. Partially completed, illegible, or mechanically reproduced entries will not be accepted. Sponsors are not responsible for lost, late, mutilated, illegible, stolen, postage due, incomplete, or misdirected entries. All entries become the property of Dualstar Entertainment Group, Inc., and will not be returned.

3. Sweepstakes open to all legal residents of the United States (excluding Colorado & Rhode Island) who are between the ages of five and fifteen on October 31, 2002, excluding employees and immediate family members of HarperCollins Publishers, Inc., ("HarperCollins"), Warner Bros.Television ("Warner"), Parachute Properties and Parachute Press, Inc., and their respective subsidiaries and affiliates, officers, directors, shareholders, employees, agents, attorneys, and other representatives (individually and collectively "Parachute"), Dualstar Entertainment Group, Inc., and its subsidiaries and affiliates, officers, directors, shareholders, employees, agents, attorneys, and other representatives (individually and collectively "Dualstar"), and their respective parent companies, affiliates, subsidiaries, advertising, promotion and fulfillment agencies, and the persons with whom each of the above are domiciled. Offer void where prohibited or restricted by law.

4. Odds of winning depend on the total number of entries received. Approximately 525,000 sweepstakes notifications published. Prize will be awarded. Winner will be randomly drawn on or about November 15, 2002, by HarperEntertainment, whose decisions are final. Potential winner will be notified by mail and will be required to sign and return an affidavit of eligibility and release of liability within 14 days of notification. Prize won by minors will be awarded to parent or legal guardian who must sign and return all required legal documents. By acceptance of the prize, winners consent to the use of their names, photographs, likeness, and personal information by HarperCollins, Parachute, Dualstar, and for publicity purposes without further compensation except where prohibited.

5. One (1) Grand Prize Winner wins a Mary-Kate and Ashley Fun in the Sun Gift Pack, consisting of the following: a portable stereo, MARY-KATE AND ASHLEY GREATEST HITS and GREATEST HITS II music CDs, Mary-Kate and Ashley beach towel, Mary-Kate and Ashley beach ball, Mary-Kate and Ashley T-Shirt, Mary-Kate and Ashley brand sunglasses, an autographed Mary-Kate and Ashley summer reading library of five books, beach hat, beach bag, glitter lip gloss. Approximate retail value: $450.00

6. Only one prize will be awarded per individual, family, or household. Prize is non-transferable and cannot be sold or redeemed for cash. No cash substitute is available. Any federal, state, or local taxes are the responsibility of the winner. Sponsor may substitute prize of equal or greater value, if necessary, due to availability.

7. Additional terms: By participating, entrants agree a) to the official rules and decisions of the judges, which will be final in all respects; and to waive any claim to ambiguity of the official rules and b) to release, discharge, and hold harmless HarperCollins, Warner, Parachute, Dualstar, and their affiliates, subsidiaries, and advertising and promotion agencies from and against any and all liability or damages associated with acceptance, use, or misuse of any prize received in this sweepstakes.

8. Any dispute arising from this Sweepstakes will be determined according to the laws of the State of New York, without reference to its conflict of law principles, and the entrants consent to the personal jurisdiction of the State and Federal courts located in New York County and agree that such courts have exclusive jurisdiction over all such disputes.

9. To obtain the name of the winner, please send your request and a self-addressed stamped envelope (excluding residents of Vermont and Washington) to TWO OF A KIND Fun in the Sun Sweepstakes, c/o HarperEntertainment, Attn: Children's Marketing Department, 10 East 53rd Street, New York, NY 10022 by December 1, 2002. Sweepstakes Sponsor: HarperCollins Publishers, Inc.

The Ultimate Fan

mary-kate

Don't miss a

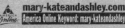

Reading Checklist

andashley

single book!

**It's
What
YOU
Read.**

- ❏ It's a Twin Thing
- ❏ How to Flunk
  Your First Date
- ❏ The Sleepover Secret
- ❏ One Twin Too Many
- ❏ To Snoop or Not to Snoop?
- ❏ My Sister the Supermodel
- ❏ Two's a Crowd
- ❏ Let's Party!
- ❏ Calling All Boys
- ❏ Winner Take All
- ❏ P. S. Wish You Were Here
- ❏ The Cool Club
- ❏ War of the Wardrobes
- ❏ Bye-Bye Boyfriend
- ❏ It's Snow Problem
- ❏ Likes Me, Likes Me Not
- ❏ Shore Thing
- ❏ Two for the Road
- ❏ Surprise, Surprise

- ❏ Sealed With a Kiss
- ❏ Now You See Him, Now You Don't
- ❏ April Fools' Rules!
- ❏ Island Girls
- ❏ Surf, Sand and Secrets

so little time

- ❏ How to Train a Boy
- ❏ Instant Boyfriend
- ❏ Too Good To Be True
- ❏ Just Between us

- ❏ Never Been Kissed
- ❏ Wishes and Dreams
- ❏ The Perfect Summer
- ❏ Getting There

Super Specials:

- ❏ My Mary-Kate & Ashley Diary
- ❏ Our Story
- ❏ Passport to Paris Scrapbook
- ❏ Be My Valentine

Available wherever books are sold, or call 1-800-331-3761 to order.

Mary-Kate and Ashley Sweet 16

Never Been Kissed

BOOK 1

Mary-Kate and Ashley Sweet 16

Wishes and Dreams

BOOK 2

Mary-Kate and Ashley Sweet 16

The Perfect Summer

BOOK 3

Mary-Kate and Ashley Sweet 16

Based on the hit Movie
GETTING THERE

GETTING THERE

BOOK 4

It's
What
YOU
Read.

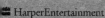

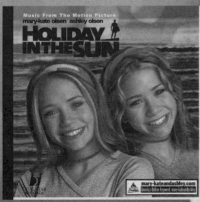
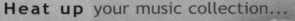

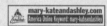